AN UNEXPECTED VISITOR...

It was a boy, a young man, dressed as black as the priest. He stumbled and turned, looking over his shoulder, then took one backward step down the runner from the door. As if realizing where he was, he spun on his heel, squaring his back to the door, and ran, sprinted, stretching his legs down the aisle towards the altar. Father Owen was about to call out, had his hand raised in protest. The boy's eyes were wide, wild, and red. His black denim jacket flapped as he bent forward and reached out with grasping fingers.

The boy reached the bottom step, stretched, then fell, or stumbled, and as he grabbed at the folds of the white cloth on the altar he half-choked, half-gasped one word. But it was heard clearly enough as its whisper rolled and filled the space of the small chapel like a small, spreading wave.

"Sanctuary!"

And then he was gone.

The scripture quoted on page 1 is taken from The Holy
Bible, King James Version, Cambridge, 1769.

The Hour And The Thief
A Novelette of The Same Strange World
by Robert J. Schulenburg
Copyright © 2011 Robert J. Schulenburg

Same Strange World Press
PO Box 43652
Tucson, AZ 85733-3652

ISBN-10: 0-6155263-7-3
ISBN-13: 978-0-6155263-7-9

Printed in the United States of America

Book Design by Robert J. Schulenburg

First Edition: August, 2011
10 9 8 7 6 5 4 3 2 1

DEDICATION

This book is dedicated to that specific woman
Who constantly challenges me to be a better man-
The man I want to be.

The Hour And The Thief

- A Novelette of The Same Strange World -

-

Robert J. Schulenburg

The Hour And The Thief

-

"I will come on thee as a thief,
and thou shalt not know what hour
I will come upon thee."
Revelation, 3:3

It was after midnight, and the chapel was empty. Father Owen knew this because the bells had rung in the tower above. Candlelight flickered against dusty windows in a vain attempt to escape the stained glass that was too dirty to let anything but the brightest sunlight through. He swept, and he dusted, and he scrubbed. These chores usually fell to the altar boys or the most junior of the clergy in residence. But it was the beginning of summer holiday, and Father Owen was, after all, the most junior clergy. In fact, he was the only clergy at present as the Monsignor and Old Father Mark had conspired to take a mid-week retreat into the hills to avoid the city's heat. With the ringing of the bells, it could only be midnight, and the chapel could only be empty.

Tomorrow, Father Owen considered, he would have to get the ladder and finally do something about those windows.

It was small, even by the standards of chapels, which are assumed to be small. Twelve rows of backed, unpadded bench-pews to either side of an aisle faced an altar raised up three steps over the audience. The white cloth was freshly clean and laid over the altar's marble tabletop.   He had done that around eleven o'clock, according to the bells. The accoutrements of the Litany and the Eucharist were assembled as well.   Gold and silver had been polished (around ten) and the floor mopped (nine).

He laid the runner up the aisle from the bottom of the first step to the double doors that led to the small courtyard whose wall kept the street away.   He pulled the pews back into position and began to run the oilcloth over them once more for the sake of dust, not polish, before going to bed.

He had had a mind to see to the cleaning of the chapel for some months now, but could never seem to find the time. The seniors had always had something for him to read or do or carry. Never preaching. No not that. He had been at St. Jude's (*How many small, urban chapels around the world were called St. Jude's?* he had often wondered since coming here.) for eleven months and two weeks. Even though he had spent most of the past two days cleaning or sorting, he felt more like a priest than he had for almost a year of serving as dogbody to the seniors.   There was something to putting the old place in order that suited his mentality. There was something to straightening the rows and beating the rugs that made him feel that he was contributing to the church in a way he wanted to but hadn't been allowed to for all this time. And it was such a little church.

He was working the third pew on the right when he heard a thump at the doors in the back of the chapel. He looked up from where he bent over the pew, his right knee on the bench cushioned under a bunched-up wad of his own cassock. *What was Gregory doing?* The older boy, Gregory, would come through the service entrance in the back if he needed anything, but should have been in bed by now with his work done for the day. There was a rattle, then the door pushed in as a bundle in black came out of the shadows.

It was a boy, a young man, dressed as black as the priest. He stumbled and turned, looking over his shoulder, then took one backward step down the runner from the door. As if realizing where he was, he spun on his heel, squaring his back to the door, and ran, sprinted, stretching his legs down the aisle towards the altar. Father Owen was about to call out, had his hand raised in protest. The boy's eyes were wide, wild, and red. His black denim jacket flapped as he bent forward and reached out with grasping fingers.

The boy reached the bottom step, stretched, then fell, or stumbled, and as he grabbed at the folds of the white cloth on the altar he half-choked, half-gasped one word. But it was heard clearly enough as its whisper rolled and filled the space of the small chapel like a small, spreading wave.

"Sanctuary!"

And then he was gone.

As his fingers touched the fabric, as the word left his lips, he was not there any more.

There was no flash. There was no bang. There was only the absence of the boy. It was like a light was flicked on, taking away a curious shadow. Father Owen blinked.

What boy? Boys just don't run into churches and then cease to be. Father Owen didn't know what just happened, but it must have not happened. The fold in the altar cloth must have been pulled when he himself had lain the runner down. He'd have to fix that when he straightened the carpet at the foot of the dais that one of the pews must have rumpled when he was manhandling them back into place.

Then he felt the chill.

He turned and looked at the open door. There was no wind, but there was a cold night air rolling in. He walked up the aisle and stood in the opening. More disturbing than what he'd seen so far, he looked across the courtyard and saw that the gate had been rolled back and streetlight showed little rivers of light in the gutters beyond. He had locked that just after eight o'clock. From the inside.

He went back into the chapel for a candle and returned to the courtyard to bring the gate back into place. He threw the bolt, then pulled it out and threw it again. As he circled the courtyard peering into shadows the bells in the tower struck one o'clock.

Up way too late, and obviously fatigued, Father Owen resolved himself to stay up a little longer to make sure the grounds were secure. That would be all for him, if the seniors returned to find the place overrun with criminals, breaking in to loot the place, take over the rectory, clean out the larder. Old Father Mark would have a fit if his cupboards came bare when he returned.

No lights shown from any of the buildings in the compound, and no noise breathed from any corner he passed. Indignation supplanted fear as Father Owen stalked through the schoolhouse and the rectory. He made his way through the kitchens, checking the locks on the pantry to quiet his fears of facing another of Old Father Mark's near-stroke rants. The locals said he could make his face turn at least three colors at once-pick your favorites. Father Owen returned to the chapel building and replaced the candle on the altar where he had pulled it.

He considered the long taper for a while, staring at the dancing flame, and frowned at how the traipsing around outside had worked his candle down, and upon being replaced, had skewed the symmetry on the altar. The candle that had stayed safe inside burned stately, tall, and noble. Its wayward counterpart guttered, flared, and honestly, looked a mess.

Father Owen liked patterns. He liked symmetry. He took comfort from things being ordered. He could replace both candles tomorrow night before the Monsignor returned for sermons Friday. He straightened the cloth absently and smoothed the carpet with a toe. He walked back to the third pew, where he had left the oilcloth, and was about to head to bed, when he heard a thump at the door.

He froze.

A rattle, just like before.

The door pushed in, just like before.

The same boy, no, young man, came sliding in from out of the shadows. Just like before.

Father Owen stared transfixed, unable to move, unable to even raise a hand this time, as the boy turned, looked over his shoulder, stepped back, and then bolted for the altar.

Did he leap? Trip? Truly stumble? Father Owen couldn't tell. Hands reached out for the altar...

"*Sanctuary!*"

And then nothing. Again.

Simply gone. The only things left were the fold in the cloth, and the rumple of the runner. And the echo of the whispered half-cry in Father Owen's ears. He turned, and before going to the open door, took the other candle with him from off the altar, to go close the front gate.

This was the stuff of dreams, and such dreams that would keep him from getting any rest, he reasoned. He threw the bolt three times and kicked the wheels in their runners before heading to the rectory for his bed. He stopped in the chapel to blow out the other candles before they burned too low.

Yes, a dream. He was obviously dreaming about finishing the night's work and got caught up in some slice of self-therapy he'd probably have to confess to Old Father Mark. Sticking to the cycle of fevered hallucinations, his nighttime ramblings would only leave him spent in the morning. Best, he figured, to put himself in his own space and leave no room in his slumber for any fancy.

He blew out the candle and went to sleep.

* * *

So why was the taper from the altar in his room when he woke up Thursday morning?

Father Owen rolled out of bed as the bells tolled seven. He washed and shaved and headed for the chapel. He couldn't remember if he'd put the cleaning supplies away when he was done with the pews last night. He couldn't remember anything up to the point that the dream took over.

Obviously he had brought the candle up, but couldn't figure why. He brought it with him, checking in the courtyard to make sure the gate was still shut. The bolt was solid and the wheels were set in the muddy grooves of morning just before the sun broke through the fog.

He came about into the chapel through the service entrance and paused to consider the remaining candle on the altar, burnt lower than the one he held, and dribbled as if it had been carried about. Stunned, without any answers, he put the candle back, smoothed the carpet with a shuffle, and twitched the altar cloth back into place. He walked numbly back to the third pew, and sat next to the oilcloth, hands on knees, and just stared ahead.

A thump at the door. He shut his eyes.

A rattle. He bent his head down, baring his neck to the rear of the chapel.

A chill on his neck as the doors opened cold morning into the small space.

Shuffling of feet. Father Owen hunched his shoulders as if they could cover his ears so he wouldn't have to hear to running steps down the aisle.

If he could have pried his hands from his knees he would have held them to the side of his head so he couldn't hear the cry.

"*Sanctuary!*"

When he opened his eyes, the chapel was empty.

With a toe for the carpet, a pinch for the cloth, the oilcloth in hand, and the last two rows of pews going undusted, Father Owen headed for the shed around in back of the rectory. He fished out his keys, and left the door open so that he could ferry the buckets, scrub brushes, mop and broom, back into their storage spaces. Leaving the ladder inside, he locked the shed as the bells tolled eight in the morning, and went to the rectory.

There were only a few clocks around the grounds. A tall brown grandfather stood in the parlor of the rectory. There was a wall clock in the kitchen. Otherwise, there were no timepieces to speak of. Old Father Mark disapproved in principle of there being a clock anywhere in the line of sight of a churchgoer, and the Monsignor kept his schedule with the tolling of the bells.

But, under his bed, in a small leather kit he had brought with him from seminary, Father Owen had secreted away a wristwatch that he kept wound and in good repair. It was a gift of his aunt's upon his receiving the rite of Holy Order. She said it had belonged to his father, and though he doubted that, he kept it to honor her good wishes for him.

There was no use for it here though, at St. Jude's. Neither of the seniors wore watches and he was expected to learn from their example in every way. So he cared for it, tucked away as it was, secret, under his bed.

He fumbled with the band, working the strap on for the first time in over eleven months. Father Owen looked at himself in the mirror, and changed out of his long cassock and into a pair of dark heavy pants and shirt. He pulled a black jacket out of the wardrobe and replaced it with the cassock. Afterwards, he went downstairs, out the parlor, and into the courtyard. He closed the gate, again, not bothering to bolt it this time, but went inside the chapel and closed that door behind him too. He sat down in the third pew and waited.

Thump. Rattle.

He turned in his seat to watch the young man pull himself around the door, desperate to put the church between him and whatever it was outside. The youth looked over his shoulder as he sidestepped into the chapel, then turned and sprinted, again, for the altar. The young man's eyes were fixed on the dais, on the instruments laid out for the Eucharist. His eyes were just as wide, wild, and red as before. Father Owen realized that the youth didn't see him, that his eyes were fixed too firmly on the altar as he dove, reaching, gasping.

"*Sanctuary!*"

And then, again, nothing.

He looked at his watch. 8:37.

Father Owen, as a student, had studied mathematics before seminary; back when he was a boy, probably no older than the youth who kept upsetting his reality. Really only less than ten years ago he conceded. His mind ran in the familiar straits of order that geometry and statistics brought. He reveled in the security and objectivity of maths. If God was Why, young Owen reasoned, then Math was How. He thought about all this as he rose to straighten, once again, the altar cloth, and smooth the runner.

One concept he remembered from an obscure course in statistics he had taken (just for the fun of it) one summer, stuck in his mind: One data point was an anecdote. Two were a trend. Three, a pattern. And patterns could be traced- forwards or backwards.

Instead of closing the chapel door, again, Father Owen went out the back service door and into the shed. He came out with the large push broom, and locked the door behind him out of habit. He came back through the chapel and closed that door behind him too. He crossed the courtyard in the persistent gloom of morning. He stepped into the street beyond the gate, and rolled it absently closed behind him, to shut the churchyard away from the city.

He had read somewhere, in a magazine, or fortune cookie, or somesuch, an old Yiddish proverb, 'if everyone sweeps in front of their house, then the whole street is clean." He stooped to work at one end of the block, at the corner of the wall, so he could play at simply going about his chores while he waited to see if he was right.

The street was grimy, but that was to be expected. It was little more than a broad alley that most automobiles wouldn't risk coming down. The bells rolled nine o'clock as Father Owen pushed his broom down the paving stones, and he paused a moment to adjust the time on his wristwatch. Yellow mold-light reflected the streetlamps in iridescent puddles. The sky overhead was turning from a dark haze to a black gloom.

Foot traffic came and went around the bends in the alley marked by the wall of the churchyard, mostly hooded marms heading to and from the shops. A few of them nodded hello as he worked his way along the wall. *Why isn't there any such thing as a clean puddle? Why is mud always involved?*

Almost none of the ladies spared a word for the priest, so he kept his head down and kept waiting, paying attention to the ends of the small streetway as he reached the gate in the middle of the wall. He stood straight and looked back at his work. He was making fair progress, and would have to remember to come back later to finish, but it was 9:30, so he leaned his broom against the wall next to the gate, and made to watch both exits from the little backstreet at once, as best he could.

Off to his left, as his back was to the wall, the alley turned a sharp corner. To the right, a t-intersection provided more scenery and more pedestrians to keep an eye on. That wouldn't be a problem however, as the sound of running feet came from the left before the youth broke around the corner, skidding in a puddle and throwing up yellow sparks of water droplets to stain the far wall darkly. His elbows flung for balance in the way only a teenage boy can manage at speed. Turning somehow on the ball of one foot and the heel of the other, he bore down on the priest.

Father Owen held up his hands, braced for impact, but the scraggle in black denim heeled to a panting stop, head down, hands on knees, shoulders heaving with the pounding of his heart and each gasping breath. He looked up through black bangs at the priest, whose hands now seemed raised ridiculously in surrender.

Father Owen was caught by the eyes that looked at him. They were both terrified and hooded with hope in that wide, wild, and red, way he had glimpsed from the third pew. He was at an absolute loss what to do, now that he was faced with his working theory working. *Is this how Newton felt when he theorized the atom? What do you do with the spaces in-between?* There were smudges of ash and what could have been blood on the lad's cheeks, on his upper lip, and under his chin. There were the shadows of tear streaks on his face, in the hollows of those eyes.

"Well?" The boy panted.

Well, what? The atom never looked back and said 'well?'. Father Owen looked around and saw the closed gate. He put his shoulder to it and began rolling it back. "In here, I guess," he grunted. And then thinking he should add something helpful, "Take the door on the left, the one on the right sticks horribly in the damp."

The boy saw the wooden double doors revealed as Father Owen rolled back the gate to expose the courtyard of St. Jude's to the street. They formed a pointed arch, and were carved with the simple motif of three crosses on Calvary He took one step forward, then surged across the courtyard towards them as Father Owen shouldered the wheeled gate into its stopping-rut.

"My left! The *other* left!" The left as you look from the dais as the seniors lead mass.

It was too late. The boy had slammed his shoulder into the door on the courtyard's left, and cursed something Father Owen didn't want to bother making out. He rolled across to the other door. This one he tested by shaking the handle, then pushing through easily into the chapel, the boy disappeared into the candle-flickered gloom inside.

"Sorry!" Father Owen called after, but wasn't sure if the boy had heard him.

Father Owen realized he had two options at this point. He could wait to see if he came out any of three times to close the gate. Or, he could close the gate and confound his dreams from the night before (*were they dreams then?*), and wait for the boy to come around the corner to play it out again.

They hadn't offered quantum physics at the seminary; the elective coursework was very restricted that way. If they had, Father Owen was sure he'd be open to other possibilities that just weren't making themselves obvious in this situation. The only logical solution, therefore, was to run away altogether.

Leaving the broom leaning up against the wall of the courtyard, and glancing back at his unfinished work in the half-swept alley, he put his back to the thoroughfare and headed around the corner from where the adolescent had come.

This stretch of narrow street, alley, was just as grimy as the first. He walked slowly, noting the sides of buildings and courtyard walls that framed the channel of muddied paving stones under the still-black sky. Occasional mist turned into weak rain, but no thunder rolled and the clouds revealed by the parting of the morning mist held in the vast bulk of the promised downpour. The air stayed brisk and Father Owen turned up the collar of his jacket against the cool.

When he reached the first four-way intersection, he could just hear the bells tolling ten o'clock. He peered ahead into the alleyway he was working his way down, and spied another opening leading to a space between two buildings that ran away from St. Jude's, parallel with the intersection he was standing at. He moved toward that opening, and took up a position just between the two passageways. Either the boy would come running down the length of the street Father Owen was on, or come out of one of the two alleys he now had a vantage point for. He waited.

The foot traffic had dried up, leaving Father Owen alone in the channel between the buildings. He was in what would be called a slum in most other cities, but was thought of as just an 'Old Quarter' here. Off and away from the church were tenements, shops, and the belts of wealthier old homes that held their own against the press of factories, warehouses, and abandoned hollow buildings.　　The river and the highway held this part of the city close together, holding itself tight.

St. Jude's was a vestige of a time when there was more space in the ghetto.　It, at one time, stood away from the manors and hostels and stables of the well-to-do.　That was back before you could see the sky without having to look straight up.　Since then, the church had wrapped itself up in its walls to hold ground against the city that closed in around it.

He stood, and he waited, alone and ignored by the city he had entered back into.

The boy ran out of the four way intersection and swung to his left towards the church.　Father Owen had become drowsy with the mist and his thoughts so that he almost missed it when it happened; almost ignored it as a normal part of the bustle of the city.　He stared after the boy and watched him make the last turn to the back street by the gate.

He began walking up the narrow street after where the lad had come this time.　This lane was just as tight as the one he'd come through, just wide enough for three men to walk side by side comfortably.　The sky was definitely black with churning clouds now.　The streetlamps were still lit to keep the dark back just slightly.

But they were few and far between on this stretch.　Father Owen peered down each opening or dark doorway as he passed, stopping to explore, only to find that doors were boarded up or alleys were choked with trash or barricades that seemed undisturbed.

Of course, Father Owen mused, the gate to St. Jude's was always shut, one way or another, before the lad had gotten into the churchyard.　He couldn't be certain that there would be any evidence of the youth's passage down these blocked alleys or out of these dark doorways.   That was, of course, considering the lad hadn't passed through yet.

Father Owen was seriously thinking about heading back, just before reaching the end of the main passage he was working his way down. He could make out two alleys, just to either side of the narrow street, almost opposite each other. The closer one to him led between the back of a store and a large brick building that could have been a modest block of homes. A few dozen yards beyond, there was the glow of lamps on a more conventional street that acted as a firebreak between the mostly abandoned ghetto of St. Jude's and the similar neighborhoods beyond.

His view was blocked however, by a large shadow that creaked and swayed between pools of lamplight, just between the alleys. Coming out of the far pool of light, the priest could just make out a series of shelves, tilted to keep fruit from rolling off, and the glint of lamplight off a sweat-moistened, bald, head.

Father Owen knew the man at once. His son worked at the school part-time in exchange for a place to study and some money to help the family. Gregory was a good lad, courteous, and promising as an academic in whatever discipline he chose to apply himself. His father, a local green grocer, was a man of simple means who put most of his savings towards finishing Gregory's education at St. Jude's.   Even though the priest had met him on several occasions, he had no desire to speak with him now, his mind occupied as it was with the mystery at hand. Father Owen ducked back down the alley and hid in the shadow of a doorway and waited for the cart to pass.

As the lumbering mass made slow, steady progress towards him, the back of the cart was disrupted like it was slammed into. The large man at the shafts held tight and let out a, "Hey!" as the youth in black denim emerged into the lamplight as he passed the front of the cart and regained his feet to speed straight down the middle of the narrow street. He had pushed himself along the side of the cart and jostled it good as he got by it, so that some of the fruit left over at the end of the day were tumbling to the ground as he went speeding by where Father Owen had hidden himself in the shadows. The priest was so startled to see the boy come out of nowhere from behind the cart like that that he didn't manage to react in any way other than to watch stupidly from his doorway as the lad shot past.

What was left behind, after the youth was gone, was the cart, slightly askew in the narrow lane with the bulky proprietor of the fruit stand picking up what was salvageable from the ground where selections of the man's wares had tumbled with the force of the roughneck's passing.

Father Owen knew that the folks in the neighborhood just called him Carter. Whether that was the family's last name or not, he couldn't say. He didn't have Gregory in any of his classes and never thought to ask the boy's last name during their brief conversations; he stuck to business with the boy, and never got that close. Father Owen always thought it funny though, that an itinerant green grocer would be saddled with the named Carter.

The big man in the shabby apron was busy putting some of the fruit back into place from where it had spilled following the sprinter's passage. He left some and didn't seem concerned about it. The cart was nearly empty anyway. Father Owen called out to the broad-waisted man as he approached, as if he was just coming on the scene and hadn't witnessed anything out of the ordinary.

"Kids today, eh Father? Shouldn't have to explain to you. Glad of the time off?" The man seemed completely nonplussed at what had happened.

"Did you know that lad, Carter? Is he from around the neighborhood?"

"Looks like one of the boys from the state house, you know? Orphan boy. I don't mind if they pinch the odd bit, especially at the end of the day, but this mad dash business is hardly necessary, wouldn't you say, Father?"

"I couldn't say," the priest replied cautiously. "It looked as though he had someplace to go."

"Ah." Carter dismissed the comment with a slapping wave. "Boys like that only have one place they need going."

Father Owen raised an eyebrow at what seemed a callous remark from such a reputable man as Carter.

"No, Father. They need be going to church. Bit of faith would do 'em a world of good. 'S why my blessed wife and I sent Gregory to St. Jude's."

Father Owen nodded. "He's been a blessing. He works hard. He helps me out more than I admit." Which was true. Gregory was almost always at hand after school to lend a hand with the chores of the church and schoolyard. Working the bells in the tower was just one of his duties. He took up that job for the Monsignor so that he'd have a place to study up in the belfry, outside the family's cramped quarters. Without Gregory, ringing the bells would be just one more task added to Father Owen's daily list of non-ecclesiastical thing to do.

"Well I'm glad he's doing you some good there Father. Working the cart alone is what I'm used to, so I don't miss him, even on holidays. But my blessed wife and I do wish he'd settle as to whether to take up the trade or not after graduation. I'd surely like to leave the business to him. This cart's got to go somewhere when I pass."

"Alone? Surely Gregory's pitching in some when he's off?"

"Off? He's off to his aunt's, he is. Stuck around long enough to get underfoot and then his blessed mum sent him west for the rest of the holiday."

"Half a moment. Gregory's in Castlebar for the summer?" Father Owen hated sounding like he was struggling to catch up with a conversation he had started. Then what Carter was saying sunk in. The summer holiday! Of course Gregory would have been gone with the rest of the students.

So, who was ringing the bells in the tower?

One mystery at a time, and if he never found out, that would be fine. *One mystery at a time.*

"Why do you ask Father?"

Father Owen grabbed an apple at random from the side of the cart and began polishing it furiously against his chest. He didn't want to think, on top of everything else he was trying to wrap his head around, who or what might be in the bell tower.

"Um, cold today isn't it? And the rain?"

Carter looked up past the streetlamps at the black sky. "Unseasonable, yes, figurin' how hot it's been." Carter smiled and nodded.

Father Owen had stopped polishing the apple against his chest and was staring at it in his hand.

"Don't mind none, Father. Eve's looked perfect, and look where that got her."

Father Owen turned the brown-red lump over in his hands. From bruise to dent it looked wholly unhealthy. Even the stem was bent crooked. "Good point. And quite a funny one too, now that you mention it."

"You know Father, you're not as much of a total git as Old Father Mark always says you are."

"Thank you. You're very kind."

"In fact, the next time he comes around the cart and starts talking about how he's going to get another stroke thanks to that milk-toast, whiny, bookworm, good-for-nothing…"

"Yes, thank you."

"Of course, Father. God fearing people we are, my family and I. Good to the church. You just keep that apple, Father. On the house."

"Again, thank you." Father Owen looked around. "I should be going."

"Late for an appointment, Father?"

"Early." He took a bite without thinking. Despite the bruise and the dent, it was quite a good apple.

"Then I won't keep you. Just heading in myself, pretty much the end of the day you know. You should come by sometime with Old Father Mark; he always finds the best pickings. But I can see you did just fine. Good day, Father."

Father Owen waved absently with the apple as the cart creaked down the alley next to the brick building, leaving only two immediate avenues for him to wait by; another alley just behind where Carter was coming from when the lad bolted past him, and a boulevard running parallel just further down where the street he was on ended. He walked down to the last intersection and set up his vigil against a walled garden that let him look back where he had come. If the youth came out the alley, he'd see him make the turn. If he came down the street from either direction, he'd turn right in front of the priest.

Father Owen chewed on his apple and waited.

Behind him he heard the muffled mid-day tones of a group of women taking their meal in the garden. Apparently the price of flour was on the rise, and Mrs. Warwick was worried about the hours her husband was keeping. The heat hadn't affected the flower beds yet, and maybe the rain would keep some of the shoots to grow taller than usual.

A few people passed on errands and Father Owen found that they'd wave and nod if he gave a greeting around his chewing and eves-dropping. Some folks he recognized from earlier in the day, now returning from the shops. Others were new to him, and gave him an appraising look before smiling and tipping their hats. The foot traffic was slowing after the noontime rush to shops and cafes, and soon Father Owen was left alone on the street, under the lights and black sky, against the garden wall.

He had finished the apple and was considering whether or not he could drop it behind a bush on the other side of the garden wall without attracting any attention, when he heard running footsteps coming from the street to his right. He looked into the noonday murk and saw, his passage spaced in the streetlamps in the distance, the teenager dressed in black, running full tilt straight for the priest. Every step he pointed into a puddle sent showers of gold spraying up behind him. Every footstep was a wet heartbeat pounding the youth further onward.

Father Owen stood away from the wall and the youngster, as if coming to a decision, slowed and panted to a stop, just as he had in front of the gate at St. Jude's. Father Owen stuffed the apple core in his pocket before the lad skidded to a halt and hoped he hadn't noticed.

"I know I'm supposed to be running. I know I'm not done yet. But I need to say this."

Father Owen knelt and took out his handkerchief from the non-apple pocket. The boy looked wobbly, and was bent over his knees like he was at the gate to the courtyard. He spit into the cloth and then paused before wiping the teenager's face. It was smeared with ash, dirt, and blood. "Okay?" he asked permission.

"Yeah, fine," and squirmed only slightly as he panted and formed the words. "You need to know why I did it."

"No I don't. Not if you won't do it again."

"I did it because I could. I did it because I was angry."

Father Owen dabbed at the boy's forehead a few times with the handkerchief. Then dabbed again. "Well, did it help?"

The boy shook his head. "Nothing helped. Nothing... helped."

"It doesn't matter, my son. I know where you're headed." He checked his watch as he flicked the handkerchief at the street to throw off the flakes of blood and ash. "Keep going, as fast as you can, you'll make it."

Father Owen only thought of the deadline the boy had to meet to get to the chapel by thirty-seven past the hour. That was almost assured now, if the boy just kept up his speed. "Just go, as fast as you can. Run and you'll make it."

Thunder rolled overhead, but there had been no lightning.

Just the flicker of hope crossed the lad's face as Father Owen squeezed his shoulders with both hands and looked him not quite in the eyes. The eyes were still too wide, wild, and red. But, he would make it. Father Owen knew that. It was a matter of math at this point.

"Go on boy, hurry!" Father Owen encouraged him. He could sense the youth responding to his positive energy and hoped the lad wouldn't guess that the priest was, in fact, still almost wholly ignorant of what was going on.

No matter. As the youth took off in the direction the priest nudged him, Father Owen knew that he had finally done some real bit of church work. He said the right words and wore the collar and was definitely, literally, a priest to look at.

The rest would be downhill. He saw where the boy was coming from. He'd have to follow a little more to close some of the gaps in the conversation. He had obviously been recognized, so he would have to be seen again before heading back. That seemed to make sense.

This was strange, sure enough, but easy. And as an adventure went, he was sure it was almost over. He may even be able to get to the windows in the chapel before the seniors returned.

He didn't know how to take that. *Adventures didn't clean the church windows*. And this was far outside his sphere of experience. However, he had been granted his prayers and given a chance to *be* a priest. He certainly seemed to be making a priestly difference in this boy's life, at least.

It hadn't occurred to him how much he was missing that in his life. He had never been able to put into words the angst he'd been dealing with at St. Jude's, but this ragged, wild urchin had opened his eyes. He had felt more like a handyman, a teacher, a school nurse, and a servant, than he had felt like a priest. Father Owen was feeling good. Father Owen was feeling damn proud.

He thought about all this as he made his way along the block in the direction the lad had come from. The street narrowed again as walled yards claimed more of the path. Where paths or private roads may have once been, wrought iron gates kept the surface of the wall continuing into the foreseeable future. There was the occasional twist or jog, but no branching as he had expected.

Father Owen took his time, unconcerned about the pace of the adventure or the timetable the youth might be on now. He would get to it, it would get to him, or in any case, he didn't have to care; it would get taken care of. The pieces would fit together and he'd just have to be there to tap them into place.

The street continued to narrow and twist till it came around the backs and sides of buildings and homes that faced other roads. Still there was the occasional passerby or couple walking together. Without motorcars able to navigate these passages, everything had to be reached by foot, and most of the people that passed had packages tucked under their arms or slung across their backs.

Before reaching the next hint of a fork in the alley, Father Owen heard running footsteps from up ahead and he composed himself so that he could speak with the lad with a sensible tone, like he had before.

For a moment the teenager looked like he was going to tear right past the priest. Father Owen stood there, hands in his jacket pockets, off to one side of the street to let him pass or stop, as he saw fit. The look on the youth's face still spoke of intense fear, and something stronger; something directed at Father Owen. It still seemed as though he was going to just run by, but at the last moment, the boy pulled up short and faced the taller man.

He looked like he was about to spit blood and venom at him. Father Owen saw hatred in the younger man's balled fists. Then the hands relaxed and the lad asked, "Who is St. Jude, anyway?" The boy croaked the words through a dry throat caked with emotion.

The question caught Father Owen off guard. He pursed his lips. "Patron saint of Desperate Cases, Lost Causes... Children, and the Chicago Police Department. In the United States," he added lamely.

"Huh."

"Yeah."

"What is it when you ask the church for protection?"

"Sanctuary. Do you mean Sanctuary?" *Of course he did.*

The youth nodded. "That's me." Then, "Where?"

He was serious. There was only the hint of hope softening his words, and still that hardness in his jaw, like he was struggling with the words he'd let out of his mouth. His jaw was set, but his hands trembled. He kept bouncing on the balls of his feet like he was going to take off at any second, like with any nudge of the wind he'd become unchecked. His eyes stayed fixed on Father Owen, but his head kept twitching like he wanted to look over his shoulder but kept checking himself.

Father Owen weighed the moment. "If," he spoke slowly, remembering from an old seminary mid-term exam, "you need protection, the church is obliged to offer shelter. There is no law anymore to protect criminals. It used to be that Sanctuary, when called for by the penitent, would put you under the care of the head of that church, until they faced the charges leveled against them."

That wasn't totally accurate. The system was more complex. It involved licenses purchased from the King of England. It had a lot to do with secular law, and involved concepts like exile. But the principle was what was important; that there was safe territory for the guilty to flee, and that the church would protect its flock from predators.

The boy just nodded him on. "Where?" he repeated. Desperate, almost pleading.

The priest turned and pointed. "That way," he turned to check his orientation from the teenager's perspective, "First right, and left where it splits."

Panting, he asked again, "Sanctuary?"

Father Owen nodded, meeting the wide, wild, red eyes. "Sanctuary."

He had done it. He had convinced the lad to run to the church.

"At St. Jude's." It wasn't a question. It was a statement demanding confirmation.

"At St. Jude's."

The boy nodded again, swallowing. "Thank you Father. I think," he looked over his shoulder and swallowed again, "I think I may make it. I'm going to try."

Then he took off running. Father Owen watched him until he lost shape, black denim in the shadows finally turning into only sprinting footsteps in the dark.

That was it then. He had sent the lad on his way. Father Owen felt relieved. He felt like a priest. He was proud. He had done a service for the youth and for the church. And, he was exhausted. He looked around and found that there was a small coffee shop just down the block. He swung himself in that direction, hands still in his jacket pockets, and headed towards a late dinner, or an early supper, satisfied in a job well done.

The coffee shop was small, and only identifiable as a coffee shop by the sigil of a cup outside on the hanging sign. There was a window facing an alley, and light pouring from it in the dark afternoon, but no green awning or little tables to make you think of a coffee shop. The place was so minimally advertised and unassuming that Father Owen was almost overwhelmed with the aroma and shelter of the place. It was picture-perfect; an unexpected find on this most strange of days. As he opened the door to let the warm air into the blessedly cool day a bell tinkled over the door, right on cue.

There was no plastic furniture or laminated tabletops inside, only comfortable places to sit and talk; tables, chairs, and sofas that had been broken in over time through many conversations and quiet moments.

This was the kind of place that locals had kept open over the years, without the need of tourists or business traffic. There was a small stand for bread and cheese in the corner, and some wine on another rack. Pastries and muffins were laid out in baskets across the counter. The shop was warm, safe, and the perfect place to sit and rest and consider what had just happened.

Father Owen bought a mug of the strongest blend the young woman behind the counter could recommend and nearly regretted it when the first sip made his eyes snap open. He drank with more caution, and picked at a blueberry scone.

The lad had come into the church, seeking asylum, Sanctuary. He was looking for the priest and following the directions Father Owen was giving him as he went along. Father Owen had heard the youth's confession, after a fashion, and convinced the lad that Sanctuary was available to him, that he could be sheltered by the church.

Playing it in reverse order, proper order for the adolescent, the priest had been confronted with a young man who was in fear and ashamed. He had requested Sanctuary, and then confessed his sins. The lad ran all-out to get to the church, to break away from what had driven him to the priest, and had come to renounce what he had done as wrong.

That about brought it to a close for him, near as he could figure. He had acted the good shepherd, directing the flock towards the pen; referring the wayward lamb from his wanderings.

He couldn't explain everything. He still didn't know who was ringing the bells at St. Jude's, and that was left well enough alone today, at any rate. He couldn't figure out if Carter was caught in the loop too. Probably not. Most likely the boy was keying in on the priest's passage through the pattern that allowed the two of them to intersect along the route. It just so happened that Gregory's father had gotten in the way during that leg of the journey. Probably. That made about as much sense as anything.. He moved his thoughts along. Father Owen began to wonder if he would find the boy when he made his way back to St. Jude's after his meal.

Why did the lad ask about St. Jude?

Then it hit him. The little voice of reason that blows down pride like a hurricane asked the damning question of his self-satisfaction.

How did he know where I preached? He had mentioned St. Jude's by name.

The clock by the door rang the quarter hour. Father Owen checked at his watch and saw that the store's clock was running a mite slow. He glanced at it and then stood up abruptly. His leg jostled the table as the chair screeched back and black coffee sloshed over his splayed fingers as he leaned forward, mouth open.

Out the window in the front of the shop he watched the young man run out of the space between the buildings across the street, leaning into the right turn to take him down the street and out of the window's view.

"Something wrong Father?" the coffee girl asked, looking up from behind the counter.

"Yes, no." He fumbled with napkins to wipe the table and his hands. He replaced the lid on a sugar bowl that had slid off when he almost upturned the table. "Excuse me," he called over his shoulder as he grabbed his jacket and ran to the door.

When he got to the street, the black figure was nowhere in sight. Neither was he, *thank God*. He had been too slow; slow getting to the street and slow in the head. But he knew where he was going now. Knew he was still going. Father Owen returned to the coffee shop and drained the last of his mug in one long pull.

He had more work to do.

As he made his way down the alley, the bell from the coffee shop ringing good-bye from behind him as the door closed, Father Owen had to admit that he didn't know what he was to do next. He'd thought he'd played out the formula. The sinner had come to him, sought guidance, repented, and been sent on his way to a safe place. What was there left to do? Why was he still going down this road?

This had turned from a puzzle, into a theory, and then into an adventure. And now it was looking more like a murky shadow of uncertainty waiting around some corner down a dark alley. He did not like it one bit.

But he ran on.

The alley wound through buildings till he got far into the center of the blocks of the neighborhood. No other alleys branched off that weren't dead ends. He made his way, peering around possible intersections and keeping his ears open for the sound of running feet. He finally came to another 'T' intersection where he had to stop and wait. He checked his wrist. 2:55. The minutes dragged, and the priest waited.

The storming current of toe to pavement echoed thinly down the alley, and Father Owen couldn't tell from which branch the boy would come, or how soon. It was like waiting for a gust of wind or a sharp noise.

Father Owen braced himself in the middle of the alley, but stood uncertainly. He wasn't sure what to expect this time around. He didn't know what questions he'd be asked, or what he'd have to say. He'd taken the boy's confession, after a fashion (he still didn't know what the confession was for. *Did it matter if the priest was willing to forgive?*), and sent him on his way to St. Jude's, as he obviously was meant to go, but what now? What had he done first?

The sound of panting breath came with the footsteps from down the alley straight in front of him. Father Owen wondered at the stillness of the dark day, and not for the first time at the strangeness of what he had become immersed in. The young man in black denim came running up on him and Father Owen tried his priestly best.

"Keep running boy!"

He tried to be encouraging like he had back at the boulevard near where he had talked with Carter. He stood in the alley with his hands spread benevolently, and put on a smile. "You're doing fine lad. Keep running." He had to admit, that even to him it sounded hollow. He put his arms down watched the panting kid.

"Of course I'm going to keep running. If I don't I'm dead."

"I…" Not knowing what to say, the priest put it back on the lad. "You know that God is with you."

"Do I?" The teenager almost choked in shock at Father Owen's lameness. He looked behind him as if to indicate that something else was with him too. "Ha! All I've got with me is a crazy priest who isn't making any sense or saying anything worth listening to, other than to tell me to run. Do I look that stupid?" He was working himself up, almost becoming irrational. "If I don't I'm dead," he said again.

"It'll be okay," Father Owen began again, completely at a loss and unprepared for the anger being directed on him, "I know…"

The adolescent was stabbing the air in front of Father Owen with his finger. His mouth formed a black hole in his face as he yelled, "You don't know shit about me! You don't know what it's like to lose a family! You don't know what it's like to live in some shithole with a bunch of criminals. You don't know what it's like to be so desperate you'll try anything to make it all stop or make it go away! You don't know what it's like to have it all blow up in your face!"

He was screaming.

And for just a moment, Father Owen's eyes got wide, wild, and red.

Owen didn't mean to slap the boy. Except that he *had* meant to slap the boy. Grabbing him by the jacket in bunched fists afterward and pulling him up off the ground to stare at him in incoherent, undirected fury- that probably surprised them both too. The youth's toes scraped the pavers, scrabbling just out of reach of leverage. Father Owen absolutely couldn't think of anything to say, so he settled on muttering, "Just shut up, just shut up, just shut up," over and over again.

"What kind of priest are you? How can you hit someone and call yourself a priest?" The scraggly youth hung like a rag doll, spat, and squeaked, and fussed.

Owen frowned tightly. "As a priest I would have trouble with it. As a sinner I seem to be doing just fine." He unclenched his jaw and loosened his grip. There was no intimidating this boy. He was running from something scarier than Owen could make himself, and they both knew it. "Look, you don't know me and I don't know you. Don't tell me what I haven't lost and what I wouldn't know about and I won't insult your intelligence either."

"You are the most damned craziest priest I've ever heard of." The youth sprayed a mist of blood as he talked through a split and swelling lip. "Where do you preach at? Our Lady of Corporal Punishment? The Blessed Virgin of Slap The Children?"

Owen just sighed and pointed back past him. "St. Jude's. Down there and left at the cafe. That's where you're headed. But hurry," he flipped his wrist to check the watch face, "You're running out of time."

He had meant to say, 'running late', but the damage was done. The boy's eyes went wider, if that were possible, and the terror settled back into him properly. He was gone with a muffled, "git," from a jacket sleeve that wiped at dripping blood, and Owen trudged down the street towards the next bend in the path.

Owen wandered down the alley, stomping through the mud puddles as he went. He breathed heavy through his nostrils air that didn't quite frost smoke out his nose. It had stayed unseasonably cool all day, but his blood was still up and his face was hot.

Stupid. Stupid. Stupid.

What the hell had he done? At the end of the day, that is what it all came to. He gets yelled at by some teenager, and he loses all sense of self, and acts like a bully.

He headed in the direction the young man had come from, not wanting to turn around and return to the church, not wanting to follow the adolescent. He hoped that this way would lead him to someplace where he could be by himself, sit, and think. He had no desire to be with anyone else- people, phantoms, or otherwise- at the moment.

The clouds rolled overhead to announce his mood, his frustration, his anger, his self-deprecation. He considered his own incompetence.

He continued to trudge through the alley as it wound, until it finally spit him out on a street facing a row of empty warehouses and factories which were like many in this quarter. They were nothing but tinder and ruin.

Owen picked a direction, right or left, he couldn't say, and followed the block. He found himself out in proper streets, and wandered aimlessly, mad. He was looking for streetlights, which might indicate the presence of people, or civilization; wary of one, seeking the other.

There was one light he spied down a bend in the road and he headed towards that, thinking it would take him in the direction of a more conventional neighborhood. It wasn't a streetlight after all. It turned out to be a lantern hung out over a wooden door, set into an old wooden structure. This was not as common in this part of the city, and Owen was struck with the sense of age about the place. The windows were blacked out and there was no light coming from under the door, but he could hear soft noises from inside through the glass. It was unmistakably a pub.

Owen went inside.

"Bit early for you?" The bartender started in without even looking, and as he continued to polish the glass he was holding he brought his eyes up, "Father?" He frowned, concluding his greeting.

Owen could imagine the white of his collar sticking out against the black of his clothes, even in the shadows, a halo tight around his neck. He loosened it, and as it came away he said, "Just stepping in out of the cold."

"We don't usually get… your kind in here Padre. Mind you don't bother the customers and you're welcome at the bar."

Owen couldn't place the dark-skinned man's accent, but the message was clear. He put the collar in the pocket of his jacket, next to the apple core, and sat down on an empty stool. There was only one other patron at the bar, a young man down near the other end. In the rest of the dark common room Owen could make out shapes in some of the booths, but nobody paying him any attention. Without asking, the bartender set a dark bottle in front of him, and a frosted glass.

"Long day?"

"Can't tell if it's just beginning or just ending."

The bartender nodded slowly. "Those are the worst." A telephone rang in the back and the bartender looked away. "Be right back."

Owen drank the first beer he'd had, not counting communion wine, since before seminary, and without even thinking about it. He was done when the bartender returned. Fortunately, he had brought a fresh bottle with him.

"Wanna talk about it?"

Owen just stared. The bartender shrugged, and propped an elbow against the bar so he could lean an ear towards the man in black as he polished another glass with the same dirty rag.

"What do you do when you've lost your family? I mean, what are you expected to do?"

"What, like losing you wife and kid? Know some folks'd be happy about that." The bartender caught the priest's look and cleared his throat. "Or, like being an orphan or something?"

"Yeah. What do you do? What are you expected to do? Go on, tell me. I want to know what you think."

"Seems like I'd go to a state home, or foster care, or hopefully a school if I could, if I was left with some kind of inheritance."

"Right. If you were left with an inheritance. And if you weren't, you'd be stuck with wherever they sent you, right?"

"Stands to reason."

"And maybe you'd hate it."

"Sure."

"Maybe you'd feel abandoned. Maybe you'd feel like you needed to take some control in your life." The bartender nodded. "Maybe you'd feel you needed to do whatever you could to take matters into your own hands. Decide what your fate was going to be."

Owen continued, "Maybe you'd make choices to be safe and easy. Maybe you'd fight fights you couldn't win. Maybe you'd get mad. Maybe you'd sell out."

Owen took a long swig. "Maybe there'd be only two choices. The school you could get into, or the place you could break into. Education or crime."

"Sure." The bartender brightened, being back on familiar ground.

"And maybe you take the easy way out. What do you do with yourself? How do you live your life? How do you live with that choice? Do you run away from it the first time it blows up in your face, or do you face it?"

The bartender considered the dirty glass in his hand as he pondered the man's words. "Some thing's you can't face alone. If you're alone, like you said, you need to get help. Otherwise, there's no facing nothing. If you try, it'll just chew you up, and then what good've you done?"

Owen thumped his glass for another. "What do you do when you don't know if you can do it? Or if you've done it wrong? What if all you're doing is just running away and not doing anything?"

"I guess I'd get pretty pissed off, honestly. If, like you say, I was doing my best and then realized it wasn't right or wasn't good enough, or whatever. I'd feel pretty stupid."

Owen had nothing more to say to that. He finished his beer and waved over another. The bartender obliged, then looked him square in the eye. He spoke low, so the young blonde man at the end of the bar wouldn't have heard.

"Look, you can sit here as long as you like and pity yourself. Now, I know you weren't talking about me, because nobody comes in here and preaches to me. So it seems that you've either really screwed the pooch from your pulpit, or you just don't understand who you're talking at from up there. Or you do, and you don't like that either. Fact is though, you came in here a priest, whether you liked it or not, and you'll leave here a priest, whether you like it or not. What is it that you think your job is, anyway?"

And that was it, wasn't it? What was his job? Visions of cleaning, tending schoolyard scrapes, teaching children, helping out the seniors, they all rushed through his head. It wasn't the liturgy, and it wasn't Sunday mornings. It wasn't the respect of passersby on the streets, and it wasn't the fixed smile of ignorance. It was doing what he did because it was what was asked of him. Simple, like that. Preach the gospel; when necessary, use words.

His head swam, so he lowered it to the bar. A short night's sleep and an endless day of emotional highs and lows swept over him in protest. He finally conceded the point, and passed out.

* * *

"Get up."

The voice came again, as the bartender shook his shoulder. "Get up Father, It is Time."

Father Owen blinked unsteadily, then glanced at his watch. It was almost 11:00. Last call. So much of the day had gone by.

"Saul, what are you talking about?" the blonde at the end of the bar chirped, draining his mug of beer, ready to order one last for the night.

"Shut up Tig." This was said automatically and without distracting hime from the customer in front of him at the moment. "Father, will there be anything else?"

"No. No, I just... I ought to, I have to, be somewhere."

"Well then, you're going to need to be in a better state than that, Padre." The bartender, Saul, sighed. And with that he turned his back to the priest, who was still trying to stand without keeping one hand on the bar. He busied himself with some ingredients from under the counter that faced the priest, but he couldn't see what was happening. Saul turned back and put a small cup in front of Father Owen.

It was the size of a shot glass, but made of glazed ceramic. Owen glanced down at the dark green liquid inside and the bartender just nodded.

The priest picked it up, and just before he drank, noticed one thin, blue wisp of smoke blow away from his nostrils. There was no stopping it though, and he upended it into his mouth, swallowed.

"Oh jeez, Saul!" This, from the blonde, Tig, at the end of the bar who watched Father Owen whose face begin to rotate through different colors. He dove belly-down onto the bar so he could reach behind and pull out a small metal pail. He ran down the bar with it, holding it by the swinging handle.

Father Owen was smelling colors and noticing two or three new shades of light as he wondered if he'd ever be able to let go of the bar rail. His whole body had gone stiff as the wicked stuff hit his system. Just as Tig reached him though, everything turned sideways, and then what was inside wanted out.

It was one solid blast of vomit, fielded expertly by the blonde man who just frowned and handed the bucket over the bar to Saul, who nodded thanks.

Father Owen put his other hand back on the bar for balance, the convulsion answering his earlier question, and noticed that Saul had brought him a damp rag for him to wipe his face with, then a glass of water. His head was immediately clear. There was no fogginess, no fatigue. He was *awake*.

He dug into his pocket and put some money on the bar. Saul glanced at it before putting it into a pocket of his own. He nodded thanks to the priest, who was busy putting the collar in place, back around his neck.

"Stop in any time Padre, if you need to."

The priest smiled and said, "I could say the same for you," and moved his chin in a way that indicated his collar, now back in its place.

They nodded to each other, both knowing they would never see the other man again.

Father Owen stepped out into the colder night and made his way slowly back to the last alley he had come out. When he got there he took stock of his surroundings.

The priest was at the end of the alley, considering which direction the boy would come and if he hadn't wasted everything, slept through it all. He leaned against the wall, hands in pockets and rested on his heel, one leg braced against the bricks to his back. He glanced at his watch. 11:10.

In front of him, across the empty street was what appeared to be an abandoned factory complex in a row of factories. Backed to the street, the priest only had a view of the building's broken windows and a few unevenly spaced doorways to give him any clue what kind of place it might have once been. Now all it seemed to be was a shell testifying to lost wealth, lost jobs, and forgotten dreams.

Directly in front of the mouth of the alley was a service entrance that sat at the bottom of a landing three steps below the level of the sidewalk. The old wooden door looked sturdy enough, and proved to be, as it burst open, banging on its hinges loudly, allowing the lad Father Owen had been following to emerge at full speed into the night.

Father Owen was ready. He intercepted the boy in the street, grabbing him by the shoulders in a way that held the boy's gaze.

"What are…? How did you…?"

"It's going to be okay. Trust me. You've got to know that. I'll see to it. I promise. After you leave, I'm going to go down there and take care of whatever I need to. It's going to be okay. But I know you have to run. You have to run and you have to go now."

The words came rushing out as Father Owen committed his act of contrition. When he was done he snapped his mouth shut, uncertain what to do next. Father Owen's jaw was clenched with resolve. He was as tense as the boy was unsettled, and he only hoped that the agitation was misinterpreted by the lad to be conviction.

The teenager was hysterical. "Where? Where do I run? Where do I go? When do I stop? Will it…"

"Yes. You have to keep running." Father Owen spoke calmly and slowly. "I honestly don't know how this is going to turn out, so keep running." This last was almost spoken to himself. "And," he added, "and I may make it harder than it has to be. That doesn't have to make sense. But remember, if you keep running and always run your hardest, you'll make it to where you're going." And at the end of the day, the priest in him couldn't resist the editorial. "You have to run the race set before you." He knew that probably sounded lame, but hoped it didn't anyway. He'd need to get more practice at this sort of thing later.

But damned if the boy didn't run.

He was still scared, ready to be angry, to vent his guilt and fear at the priests he was about to meet, but he ran, sure enough. He took off down the alley in a straight line, turning only in the distance where the twist between buildings forced him out of sight.

The door was closed but not locked. Father Owen peered cautiously into the dark, but nothing came rushing out after the boy. Lightning flashed without the company of thunder, illuminating a set of rickety wooden stairs leading straight down into the darkness.

He fumbled by the door and a tiny chain brushed against his hand. He pulled on it and heard a small click as a single bulb came on in the cellar below. Father Owen took the stairs and came to a halt in a cleared space in the middle of a forgotten storeroom.

Boards, bags of what could have been fertilizer by their stink, crates of all sizes, and large metal drums, filled the space with no apparent order. Shadows were everywhere. The cellar was cold but dry in the night, and there didn't seem to be any sign of life. No rats, no cockroaches, not even spiders. There were no exits, except for a collapsed part of ceiling that left plaster and wooden beams scattered in one corner of the basement room.

There was space under the stairs where nothing had been stacked or shoved. Father Owen climbed to the top of the staircase, closed the door, and pulled the tiny chain. Once in darkness he ran one hand down the rail as he took the creaking boards one at a time with a tentative step. When he reached the dust and brick at the bottom, he kept his hand trailing the banister till he made his way under the stairs, banging his head only once as he took what he hoped would be a hiding spot that would leave him in deep shadow when the light came back on.

And eventually, it did. Father Owen hoped his collar would not stand out in the shadows under the staircase the way it had seemed to at the bar. The lad stomped down the stairs and tossed a beer bottle into the corner of the room. He dropped a backpack on the floor at the foot of the stairs and pulled out another bottle. He broke the cap off expertly on the rail, and the disc went flying back into the shadows next to the priest.

The boy sat at the foot of the stairs and muttered. He spoke too quietly to be understood, but his words were clear. He was angry. He was working himself up for something. Finally he put the bottle down, the glass was so dark Father Owen couldn't tell if it was empty or not, and pulled a book from the backpack.

It was small, brown, and covered in what looked like coarse animal hair. The pages looked like they were different colors, some black, some white, some red. Father Owen couldn't make out any of the writing from his vantage point behind where the boy was sitting.

The lad made a hunched figure on the foot of the stairs as he read it over quickly, skipping from page to page, sometimes going backwards a few pages to read something over again. Then he got up and left the book on the step he was sitting on.

The teenager moved around the room and cleared a large space near the foot of the stairs. He pulled pieces of roof timber, some stacked lumber, and scrap wood together and arranged some of them to form a five-pointed star. He moved the rest, apparently unacceptable scraps, off to the side.

Then the youth pulled out a bag of what could have been fertilizer and tore a corner free. He poured the powder around in a wide circuit that enclosed the star, forming a circular pentagram.

The boy disappeared into the darkness again and pulled out some canisters with foul smelling liquids inside, not gasoline or paint, but definitely flammable. He dribbled this on top of everything.

The lad retrieved the book from the stairs and checked it one last time. From his black denim jacket, he pulled a book of matches. He lit the powder and the wood. The flames crawled slowly over their fuel, but did eventually create the crude, blazing pentagram they promised. The light was surprisingly strong, and the fumes coming off the wood and powder were sharp and biting.

He checked the book again. Then, as if remembering something, ran up the stairs and turned off the light. Just before the bulb went out, Father Owen risked holding his watch out to check the time. 11:59.

The lad came back down the stairs and stepped into the burning circle. He stepped carefully over the burning timbers into the center pentagon formed by the crossed beams. He settled himself down, sitting on his knees like a samurai about to commit hari kari, and cleared his throat.

"My Lord Satan," the boy began, the book held open in one shaking hand in front of him as his other hand rose dramatically. The rest of what the boy said was nonsense; sometimes gibberish, sometimes blasphemy, and obviously almost beyond the boy's comprehension.

He occasionally gestured, grunted, or raised his voice in angry tones. Eventually, as the flames licked higher around his kneeling form, he stopped, and closed the book with a snap of finality.

And nothing happened.

"Pat and his stupid ideas," he muttered. "Damned stupid book. They can go to hell." He kicked at the book where he had dropped it, and its pages leaped into flame as they folded across a burning pole. Then he stalked out of the circle and kicked the stray beer bottle into a corner. He raised his voice in vicious fury at the ceiling beams and abandoned cobwebs. "Pat can go to hell. The damned orphanage can go to hell. My damn useless family can go to hell. This whole damned city can go to hell!"

"*And you, boy, can go with them.*"

The voice had come from the far side of the room, and Father Owen and the boy both whipped their heads around to face it. In the far corner, where the shadows were darkest, was the distinctly blacker shape of something bigger than a man that shifted its weight like a beast.

Where the head should be, two glowing slits allowed licking flames to dance as the shape moved. The dim light of those fires illuminated a wide forehead, dark and textured with scars or scales. The black bases of horns were visible at the temples, and the sharp cheekbones and hints of fangs were just evident against the shadows. The demon was smiling, cruel and willful.

Father Owen was stunned. The boy, unbelievably, pointed an accusing finger. It shook as he protested, "You are under my power. You're supposed to be in the circle. You have to do what I say."

*"**And just where,**"* the demon laughed, *"**does it say anything about that in that little book of yours?**"*

The youth looked stupidly back at the whisping pile of ash that had been the book of hair. It was obvious he couldn't answer the question. His legs wobbled, and he sunk to a sitting position on the floor at the foot of the stairs.

The beast laughed as it grew more real, its oppressive nature stinking through the room.

*"**Study up boy. The circle was to protect you, as a damned servant of my master. But you're not in the circle anymore, are you? Now it's little more than a pretty nightlight for me to see your face by as I tear pieces off you. Stupid, stupid, foolish, stupid boy.**"*

The beast seemed to be shrugging off blankets of darkness, as if it was emerging from some greater depth. It strained forward, but did not come out of its corner. It was like it was stuck halfway through a hole it needed to wiggle the last little bit out of. It wasn't going to be long.

Father Owen found himself standing next to the teenager. He had no notion of how he got there, other than logic dictating he must have come out of hiding to try to help the lad.

"Get up." The lad just sat there, mouth open. He grabbed the lad by the right arm and tugged at him till he got to his feet. "Get up!"

There was still no response from the would-be Satanist, other than to glance at the priest without comprehension. Shock had made him instantly sober. But he remained paralyzed by the sheer force of the evil presence working in the cellar. It sapped his strength, muddied his resolve, and instilled absolute fear. It was like being caught in headlights, or the gaze of a hunting cobra.

"Well? RUN!" He pointed up the rickety stairs.

The boy stood motionless, pinned between the priest's grip and the will of the devil in the corner that was inching slowly closer, ready to snap its unseen tether.

He stared up at the white collar around Father Owen's neck, looking so much the scared little boy who'd just been caught drawing on the walls of his bedroom. He had summoned a demon, could very well be about to die, and all he could muster emotionally to respond to the situation was a look of shock and guilt, not for what he had done, but for getting caught.

Father Owen gave a sharp tug that made the teenager's bangs sweep across his eyes. "Come on son. Think! Look at it! Look!" Father Owen grabbed the boy's chin and turned it forcibly away from him to look over at the fell shape in the darkness. "Do you have any doubt that that is a demon over there? Do you believe in Hell now?"

Father Owen leaned in and pulled the boy's attention back to him so that he'd be faced with every word. "If there is a Hell, for certain, do you think there might be a Heaven? Now think it through boy, which side's going to be the one to give a damn and help you?"

The boy raised a shaking hand, and with the awkwardness of half-remembered, unpracticed ritual, looked like he was going to begin to trace a trembling cross over his heart. His shaking finger got about half-way through and then just pointed at the priest and swallowed.

It looked like he might melt, like he might start to cry. The demon began to laugh a chainsaw laugh. Father Owen gave the arm a tight squeeze to reassure him and to hold him upright. His words came quietly but clearly in a sudden stillness as the demon stopped laughing and began moving forward out of the shadows.

"In the name of all that's Holy, run." And then the priest swung him around by the arm and flung him at the base of the stairs.

That was all he needed to get him moving. The lad caught himself on the handrail and started taking the stairs two at a time. He was up and out the door just as a metal drum crashed through the wooden steps right below the landing. As the stairs collapsed halfway up under the impact of the drum, the demon howled like a gale that was ready to break over the city.

*"**Running will make it sweet! I will hunt you first little boy, before I come for your friends, your family, your pet kitten!** "* The beast began to laugh uncontrollably.

Father Owen knew the youth had heard, even though he was well and outside the cellar now.

*"**But first, I'll feed on this little priest.**"*

And then it stepped into the open, clear of the clutter and debris and deepest shadows at the far end of the cellar.

The darker blackness behind the demon came with it, obscuring the forms of the boxes, crates, and barrels it had been standing among. There was just enough light cast by the burning pentagram to make out the sloped shoulders, horned head, and shaggy legs, bent backwards, that the beast stood upon.

Without thinking, Father Owen stepped backwards into the burning pentagram, searching for any refuge. The demon just laughed louder as it took another step forward.

"That only would have protected the boy. You had nothing to do with me being here, priest. You have no place in that circle."

Father Owen's heel kicked a timber he got too close to. It rolled up, distorting the line of the pentagram. The symbol shifted asymmetrically. His thoughts were racing and his heart was pounding. He had his hands spread wide as if he were going to catch the demon as it charged, but the beast didn't charge, and if it did it would snap him in half anyway.

The pattern of the ruined pentagram stuck in his mind. Four lines met as if to form the star, but one line ran almost parallel with the cross-piece so that it looked more like a twisted paperclip than an arcane symbol. His thoughts raced again. One line ran almost parallel with the cross-... *Oh God, could it work?*

He turned and kicked furiously at the beams that ran wide and joined the steeple of the figure with the cross-piece. They moved up easily enough, though they still smoldered and scorched his pants. They had been laid down last, and just moved on top of the other pieces or just under each other. Now he was looking at a giant flaming A, like a symbol for anarchy. One cross-piece and two timbers each for the limbs of the peak.

The demon stopped its slow but steady advance. The demon stopped laughing. It barred its teeth.

The priest's heart pounded like a hammer in his chest. His legs ached from being scorched. Sweat began to drip from his brow even as his mouth went as dry as a desert.

In his desperation Father Owen grabbed the end of one of the poles and levered it to the inside. He didn't take time to shake the soot and embers from his hands before moving to the next one to bring the steeple together. He repeated this two more times to form a crude sign of addition in the burning circle of fertilizer. He fell to his knees in the process and fury of scrambling the pieces into order.

"*Stop that.*" The hell-beast growled. The demon flexed its wings. "*You don't know what you're doing, you silly priest. Just stand still, give up, and I'll make this quick.*"

Father Owen chuckled, panting, and bracing himself for the next step. He looked back at the demon, which was tensed, watching and indecisive. "Don't know what I'm doing? Maybe. That's why they call it faith. Good thing I'm a priest then."

And with that he grabbed two of the four poles bisecting the cross-piece, and dragged them towards the demon in three long strides, clutching them to his chest and inhaling the smoke as he pulled them to lengthen the symbol to form a cross.

The demon lifted one black-clawed hand, and snarled, "*Then say your prayers little man,*" its smile was wicked and pointed, "*you're outside your circle.*"

Father Owen realized he had fallen outside of the circle. The center of the crossbeams was in the center of the circle, but he had carried himself out of its protection when he extended the length of the cross. He smiled the smile of the exhausted, burned, half-mad, and desperate. "Way ahead of you, you bastard."

He was on his knees, literally. His hands held under him so he could support himself on his elbows. He was almost bent double. And he prayed the prayer he'd been praying since realizing he was trapped in a basement with a demon.

"Please God help me. I don't want to die."

He closed his eyes and his body shook. Not even he could tell if he was laughing or crying.

"Get up."

That, was not the voice of the demon.

Had it worked?

Father Owen lifted his head and opened his eyes, only slightly, against the brightness.

The brightness of the angel.

He continued to sit up, and shaded his eyes. He could make out the white-lit outlines of support beams and crates. He could pick out the image of the demon, frozen in bright tableau against the radiance coming from next to the priest. The devil seemed to be smoking. Wisps of vapor curled up from its shadow-wrought wingtips and arm scales, as if they were being seared by the cold holiness of the being in the cellar with it.

An angel. It did work. He had summoned an angel.

"Don't be too proud, young Father," Heaven's soldier chastised quietly, **"I am here because I was needed. But yes, I did respond to your call."**

Father Owen was absolutely overwhelmed, and appropriately humbled, as his mind began to wrap around the fact that he was now trapped in a cellar with an angel and a demon.

He soiled himself, and tried to think of what he could possibly have to say to an angel. Pride was no longer an issue.

"I... I..." He wanted to say, *I believe now...I understand now...* but all that would come out was the default litany of mankind's arrogant soul. This simple testimony, wholly lacking, was all he could manage out loud.

"Yes, young Father. He knows."

Father Owen tried to stand and reached out a shaking hand for support. The angel grabbed him by the upper arm in a grip firm as rock, but not crushing like stone.

"It is not safe here young Father. I need to deal with the rogue."

Father Owen nodded dumbly.

"You need to be made safe."

Father Owen nodded again.

"Goodbye young Father."

With the gentleness of an angel, the creatures God sent to level cities and deliver plagues, Father Owen was thrown through the air, up the broken stairwell, and through the wooden door at the top of the landing.

He landed on the shoulder that took the impact of the door, and rolled for at least ten feet, clearing the steps outside and ending up sprawled in the middle of the street.

Why couldn't he have been blessed with unconsciousness? Everything hurt. Some things seemed broken. *This is what an angel meant by safe?*

As he got to his elbows and knees, he checked the wristwatch, visible under his torn sleeve. It was unbroken. The crystal face wasn't even scratched. He crawled back to the broken doorway and peered through the hole he'd made.

In the cellar, quite literally, a battle was being fought between light and shadow. As the beast stepped forward he seemed to pull the murk from the cellar corners with him. The spans of brightness that fanned from the angel's shoulders like armored wings were slapping at their tips against the hooked ends of the solid darkness that spread from behind the demon.

Words seemed to be exchanged, but Father Owen's head was still rattling with the force of his rescue. What he heard was like the conflict between enraged dolphins and frenzied sharks. Harmonics from the angel were countered with the grating of the demon's cries. The two circled as their power built in the chamber that was now much too small to contain either of their presences.

They collided, grappled, and tore at each other in a shower of black and silver sparks. It soon became too intense to watch. Father Owen scrambled backwards, trying to get his feet under him, when a scream of rage and a righteous battle cry broke from the cellar. From inside came the sound of crashing timbers and falling walls, followed by the bright shot of the agents of Heaven and Hell into the midnight sky, rolling and beating each other as they climbed higher.

The eruption appeared to be little more than the gout of flame from some factory chimney from anywhere else in this district, but Father Owen knew what he was looking at. The pair corkscrewed together into the night sky, thunder and lightning embraced and at war. At a zenith of about one hundred feet, the angel held the demon up by the throat in one hand and threw him towards the earth horned-head first, like some rotten fruit. The creature fell, howling and clawing at the angel still hovering on flaring wings. It broke back through the roof of the warehouse and Father Owen heard crashes from inside where the beast must have broken through other floors and walls within the structure. From out of the air, the angel drew a blazing sword. It flared its wings once, and dove after the demon into the ruin of the building.

Inside the old warehouse, something blew. Whether it was long-forgotten combustibles that were ignited by the fury playing out inside the building, or just the death throes of a creature of Hell, Father Owen would never know.

Instinct told him to start backing away when he saw the eruption from the roof, and when he heard the roar and saw the fire roll inside through broken windows he was afraid he'd never be able to run fast enough from the firestorm that was about to burst free into the streets. The fire tore around inside the building as untold energies were released.

When it got out, it was a sure bet that the whole quarter would go up in flames. The building seemed to swell with the potential for destruction it was about to realize. He was looking at a fireball nearly as big as a building, contained for the briefest of moments in the shell of the old warehouse like a nuclear explosion trapped inside the shell of an egg.

Father Owen was certain he was looking at the start of a disaster that would blow through the city, scour it free of the empty shells and forgotten relics that these neighborhoods represented to the mind of the modern sprawl that contained it like an abscess.

And that would be the end of everything. The end of the ghettos. The end of the families living together comfortably, creating a new community in the shadow of factory carcasses. The end of people holding on to what was theirs for generations, no matter what. The end of alleyways too small to let cars race through but big enough for a man to walk down arm in arm with his wife. The end of little coffee shops that served only locals because only locals knew where they were. The end of walled gardens. The end of a familiar craziness that he wasn't sure he wanted to give up. The end of St. Jude's.

Once this fire started, he knew there would be no stopping it until there was nothing left to burn.

Father Owen saw all this as he sat on his knees, there on the cobbles of the narrow street. He had stumbled and fell with the weight of his injuries and the fatigue of a most inexplicable day. He saw all the beauty he had never gotten to know, and saw it ready to be blown away.

Was the loss of all this worth the soul of one angry teenager?

The priest in him said, *Of course.*

Of course our choices drive us to consequences that spiral beyond us; and if we're lucky we're left unscathed and better for them. That's cold comfort to our neighbors and loved ones. The priest knew it was selfish, but for so much to be lost, when he had just found it...

Father Owen looked up at the sky and wept, waiting for the heat and fury that was barely contained in the crumbling walls of the warehouse to wash over him at any moment, to erupt like the volcano it seemed to be.

But as his hot tears streaked his face, a cool wind blew through his hair. He opened his eyes and shut them again as lightning flashed across the sky. Thunder rolled, and the heavens finally opened up. Rain, like grace, fell on the ghettos of the city, saving them from a fate they were entirely unaware of.

It soaked into his clothes, plastering them to his body. It ran the soot and dirt off of his face, and washed the smoke from his hair. It made his tears insignificant. Then it made them tears of joy, tears of relief. The coolness of the rain ran through his bones and back into his muscles. He almost fainted with the knowledge that he had somehow survived, and had somehow been changed. He sat in the street, on his knees, laughing, and crying, and laughing, and drinking in each drop that rolled into his open mouth, clean, new, and alive.

Gouts of steam erupted from the warehouse, but they were obscured in the downpour. Father Owen got to his feet and wiped his eyes clear with one wet hand. He swayed slightly, but began walking steadily enough after a few paces. There was no wind now, and the rain fell straight down on top if his head. He had only one thing left to do.

Father Owen made his way slowly through the rain-dark streets that were being sluiced clean with the unseasonable rain. In the morning it would be clear, after the fog lifted, and clean, after a fashion familiar to the locals. He walked through the rain, head held up, drops falling off the tip of his nose, and smiling.

When he got to the open gate of St. Jude's he walked straight into the courtyard. He didn't know whether he should have expected the gate to be open or not. To be fair, there was plenty he still didn't know, or understand.

He didn't know who was ringing the bells, and decided he didn't need to.

He resolved to take on simple mysteries from now on, like what day it was, and where he might happen to be at any given moment. There was too much going on in the world around him to be occupied with much else.

He paused in the archway over the open doorway, and wiped the extra water off his face and smoothed his hair. He scraped the bottom of his shoes on an obliging projectile (so he wouldn't get the runner too dirty in the aisle), and walked quietly into the candlelit chapel.

The young man was huddled at the base of the altar at the end of the aisle, one hand clutching the altar cloth in a balled fist.

"I think we need to talk."

The young man nodded. Father Owen walked into the chapel, closing the door behind him, to keep out the night's chill. He had left the gate in the courtyard open, but that was okay.

THE END

ABOUT THE AUTHOR

Robert J. Schulenburg is a native of San Jose, California. His career in Special Education has led him to serve in Central America and the Caribbean with the US Peace Corps. His study of culture, myth, and religion from around the world has heavily influenced his writing, prompting studies in how the condition of the individual influences and is influenced by the strange world we all live in.